To Charlotte
G.R.

To Johan and Jesper
I.P.

First published in Great Britain in 2005 by

Gullane Children's Books
an imprint of Pinwheel Limited

Winchester House, 259-269 Old Marylebone Road,
London NW1 5XJ

1 3 5 7 9 10 8 6 4 2

Text © Gillian Rogerson 2005
Illustrations © Ingela Peterson 2005

The right of Gillian Rogerson and Ingela Peterson to be identified as the author and illustrator of
this work has been asserted by them in accordance with the Copyright, Designs and Patents Act, 1988.
A CIP record for this title is available from the British Library.

ISBN 1 86233 579 6

Printed and bound in China

Happy Birthday Santa!

Gillian Rogerson ● Ingela Peterson

GULLANE
CHILDREN'S BOOKS

"I wonder when Santa's birthday is," said
Sylvie the Elf. She gave an apple to Rudolph.
"He doesn't have a birthday," said Rudolph.
"Have you got any carrots?"
"Everyone has a birthday,"
said Sylvie. "I'll go and ask him."

Sylvie found Santa in his house. "Hello, Sylvie," said Santa. "Do you think it's warm enough to wear my sunflower shorts?"

"When's your birthday, Santa?" asked Sylvie.
"Oh! You don't want to go worrying about that now, Sylvie," said Santa.
"Green or orange T-shirt? Mmm. I think orange is more my colour."
I'll find out when your birthday is thought Sylvie.

Sylvie went to see the Chief Elf. He knew everything.
"Do you know when Santa's birthday is?" asked Sylvie.
"Of course," said the Chief Elf. "I know everything.
I've got it written down somewhere."

The Chief Elf looked
through his diary…
in his notebook…
at his calendar…
under his desk…
and in his lunchbox!

He scratched his head.
"It might be on a Wednesday –
but I can't be sure."

Rudolph was waiting
outside for Sylvie.
"The Chief Elf couldn't
help," sighed Sylvie.
"Well, my Uncle Bert might know.
He's very old," said Rudolph.
So Sylvie and Rudolph caught the
bus to The Reindeer Retirement Home.

THE ULTIMATE REINDEER SHOE

COOL OUTFIT

Uncle Bert was taking an aerobics class. Sylvie and Rudolph waited until the class was finished. Then they waited until Uncle Bert got his breath back.

"Do you know when Santa's birthday is?" asked Sylvie.
"Absolutely…" wheezed Uncle Bert.
Sylvie and Rudolph waited.
"Absolutely… no idea!" Uncle Bert said.

On the bus journey back Rudolph stared glumly out of the window.
It was getting dark. Sylvie stood up and said loudly,
"Does anyone know when Santa's birthday is?"
"15th May," "29th July," "3rd November," chorused the animals.
"Who's Santa?" asked a small rabbit.
Sylvie shook her head. She sat down and stared even more
glumly out of the window.
Just then, a bear tapped Sylvie on the shoulder.
"The Wise Old Owl might know. You can get off at the next stop."

Sylvie and Rudolph found the Wise Old Owl
getting ready for a night out!
"Excuse me, Owl," said Sylvie. "Do you know
when Santa's birthday is?"

"No, my dear. I don't," said the owl.
Sylvie and Rudolph sighed.
"But I know how you can find out. You'll have to
come with me to the All Night Disco."

The Wise Old Owl led Sylvie and Rudolph to a
clearing in the forest, where the creatures of the night
were dancing and singing under the light of the moon.
The owl called out to the creatures,
"Who knows when Santa's birthday is?"
A bat answered, "The Two-Hundred-Year-Old
Turtle knows. But he's asleep and
we don't know how to wake him up!"

The creatures of the night decided to try anyway. They began to dance around the sleeping turtle. Sylvie and Rudolph joined in. They clapped and shouted, stomped and yelled. But the turtle didn't wake up. Rudolph whispered to Sylvie, "This is a waste of time."

At that moment, the turtle's eyes sprang open.
"Who's whispering?" he said.
Once he had woken up properly, Sylvie asked the
Two-Hundred-Year-Old Turtle about Santa's birthday.

The turtle thought…

And thought…

And thought…

"It's tomorrow,"
he said.

Sylvie and Rudolph went back
through the forest and headed for home.
"We've so much to do," said Sylvie. "First of all – the presents."
Rudolph yawned. "Can't we just send him a card?"
"Of course not," said Sylvie. "Let's go round and
see if anyone has anything we can give him…"

Sylvie and Rudolph collected
so many gifts for Santa they
could hardly carry them!

By the time they had finished, it was starting to get light.
A very tired Sylvie and Rudolph
stood outside Santa's house. They could hear him
snoring inside! They had a sack full of presents that
they had spent all night gathering and preparing.
"Now what?" asked Rudolph.
Sylvie looked up at the roof.
"I'm *not* going down the chimney!" said Rudolph.

Luckily, Santa's house was never locked!
Sylvie placed the huge pile of presents
around the plant in the corner of Santa's
living room. Then she put a card on top.
"Has he left any carrots out?" asked Rudolph.
"Don't be silly," said Sylvie.
"Come on, let's go!"

Santa TV

Rudolph and Sylvie quietly left the house.
And as Sylvie closed the front door, she whispered . . .

"Happy Birthday Santa."